This notebook is dedicated to Elise,
who came first and paved the way —
thank you!

PIGEON POST 11¢

It's a life skill
NOT to copy people.

It's even more of a
life skill to write great
reviews of terrific books
like this one.

Pleasant Company Publications
8400 Fairway Place
Middleton, Wisconsin 53562

another
life skill ⟶ Book Design by Amelia

Both boys AND girls
can read this
book.

Library of Congress Cataloging-in-Publication Data
Moss, Marissa.
Oh boy, Amelia!/by Marissa Moss.
p. cm.
Summary: Ten-year-old Amelia watches her older sister Cleo change when she
gets her first boyfriend, while Amelia takes a class in "life skills" and tries to
figure out what it means that she likes shop class better than home economics.

ISBN 1-58485-344-1 (hc.)   ISBN 1-58485-330-1 (pbk.)
[1. Sex role-Fiction. 2. Schools-Fiction. 3. Sisters-Fiction.]

I. Title
PZ7.M8535 Oh 2001
[Fic]--dc21   2001-018857

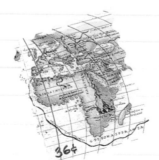

36¢

First Pleasant Company Publications printing, 2001

An Amelia® Book
American Girl® is a trademark of Pleasant Company.
Amelia® and the black-and-white notebook pattern
are trademarks of Marissa Moss.

Manufactured in Singapore

Counting is a
basic life skill,
so count for
something!

01 02 03 04 05 06 TWP 10 9 8 7 6 5 4 3 2 1

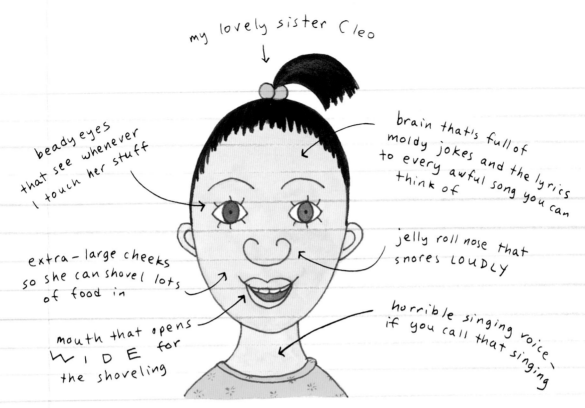

You would think anyone in their right mind would keep as far away from Cleo as possible. (I do, and I'm her sister!) You would think she wouldn't have many friends, but she does. And now she even has a <u>boy</u>friend. At least she calls him her boyfriend.

When she started gushing about this cuuuute guy named Oliver, I thought she was making him up. But he's real. I saw him with my own eyes. What's even harder to believe is that he <u>is</u> cute - <u>and</u> nice <u>and</u> smart. So why is he with Cleo?

I looked into the mirror to see if anyone would call my eyes beautiful. I think they're nice.

Anyway, I don't want a boyfriend. But it would be nice if someone thought I was beautiful.

I met Oliver when he came over to help Cleo with her science project. That was strange — Cleo's good at science, and she's never needed help before. I don't think she really wanted help anyway. She just wanted to look into Oliver's eyes. And she didn't want me around while she was gushing over him.

Cleo's warning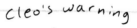

When Oliver gets here, I want you to STAY AWAY! Don't answer the door. Don't come into the kitchen and bug us. Just stay in your room.

Who did she think she was? Queen of the house? It's a free country — I can go where I want!

Of course, that meant I had to be the one to open the door. Lucky for me, Cleo was in the bathroom just when the doorbell rang.

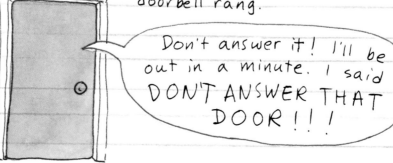

Don't answer it! I'll be out in a minute. I said DON'T ANSWER THAT DOOR!!!

I answered it.

Oliver

He **does** have nice eyes.

friendly smile

little gold earring - very cool!

backpack full of heavy science books

box full of beakers, test tubes, plastic tubing, and other neat stuff

I was going to say something clever. I was going to say something funny. But before I could say anything at all, Oliver said, "I didn't know Cleo had a little sister." Then he patted me on the head! I'm **not** little (short maybe, but not little!), and there's nothing worse than a head-pat! That's what grown-ups do to kids they want to ignore. It's like they think you're a dog.

the dreaded head-pat

There, there.

Off you go!

THINGS GROWN-UPS YOU FEEL

↑
crouching down to your size,
as if you're teeny-tiny (embarrassing!)

↑
pinching your cheek
(to be avoided at all costs!)

↑
talking in a high-pitched
singsong voice used for small
dogs and children (unbearable!)

↑
asking boring questions, the
kind they'd never ask another
grown-up (yaaaawn!)

DO TO MAKE LIKE A BABY

WAAH!

the big waxy, puckery kiss that leaves a lipstick mark on your cheek (uogh!)

Hey! How's stuff?

giving you the buddy-buddy chin-chuck (so fake!)

For you!

Gulp! Thanks... I guess.

offering a present fit for a toddler (how insulting!)

Does she like her school?

She just loves it!

talking about you as if you weren't there or can't understand what's being said (it's torture!)

So he had that colonoscopy done.

Spare me the details!

talking about other things as if you weren't there (even worse!)

O.K., there _are_ worse things than a pat on the head. But Oliver is just 13, so he shouldn't treat me like a little kid. I never got a chance to say anything, though, because Cleo leaped out of the bathroom.

Cleo ran up to Oliver.
↓

she gave me the evil eye.

she gave him the goo-goo eyes.

They started to work at the kitchen table. What a coincidence — I happened to be really, _really_ hungry just then! So I decided to make a smoothie.

First I crushed ice in the blender.
↓

WWHIRRR!

CRACK!
CRUNCH!

SMACK!
SMUNCH!

GGRRRRRINDD

I admit, it was a little noisy, but how else can you crush ice? With a hammer? After I added the yogurt and banana, naturally I needed to run the garbage disposal to get rid of the extra ice.

GGGRRAGKLE

Sssssss

Cleo, gritting her teeth and hissing at me ↓

Oliver, sweetly explaining and not annoyed at all ↓

↑ me, innocently whistling

I was going to drink my smoothie at the table, but Cleo looked ready to erupt, so I thought maybe I should go to my room after all. Then I realized Cleo <u>couldn't</u> get mad with Oliver there because that would make her look bad. So I stayed. And even worse (to Cleo), I dared to talk to Oliver.

That looks like a cool project, Oliver.

steam rising ↗

Thanks.

Then I sipped my smoothie slooooowly and pretended not to listen to him and Cleo. →

← innocent bystander face — with ears W I D E open

    I found out <u>why</u> Oliver's helping Cleo. She may be good at science, but he thinks he's even better. He's got a project in the state science fair! He made some kind of cool robot. (I'd love to see it!) I heard him ask Cleo if she wants to go with him to the awards ceremony. I wish I could go — I could meet all the winners and find out where they got their ideas. Maybe I'd even get some ideas of my own.

Cleo was acting so <u>dumb</u> around Oliver. You'd think she'd want to act smart and impress him. Instead she was just the opposite.

You mean that's how you make a circuit? I had <u>no</u> idea!

← she's known how to make an electrical circuit since she was in second grade! Why was she lying?

    After Oliver left, Cleo said that if I EVER got in the way again, she'd burn all my notebooks. I don't know why she's so sore — I was polite. But I'd better hide my notebooks just in case.

Now that I knew about the science fair, I needed to get on Cleo's good side. I tried my angel act.

unfortunately, this works better on Mom than on Cleo.

Cleo snorting at me — once Oliver was gone, she wasn't dumb and sweet anymore.

It'll be hard work being nice enough to Cleo so she's nice back to me.

I tried to apologize to Cleo about the noisy smoothie, but she was too mad at me to listen — she said I wasn't really sorry. But I am. From now on, I'll be sweet, sweet, sweet (and quiet!) when Oliver comes over.

Apology NOT accepted!

Yesterday was bad enough, with evil-eye Cleo mad at me. Today was even worse. We started Life Skills class. With a name like that, you'd think we'd learn something useful, but we won't. Instead of learning how to parachute from a crashing airplane or how to snowshoe across a glacier, we're going to sew, cook, and do carpentry and bicycle repairs. BOOOOOORING!

The teacher is Mr. Bipka.

Mr. Bipka is one of those balding guys who grows six hairs really long and combs them over the top of his head. If he was really good at life skills, he'd cut those hairs!

Boys and girls, we're going to have a lot of fun, a lot of fun.

The beard is to make up for the bald head — uh, oh, his face is upside down!

when someone has to tell you you're going to have fun, it means you probably won't.

Amelia's Life Skills Class

These are the life skills _I_ would teach!

How to dispose of toxic wastes:
↓

green beans and liver — the deadliest!

How to escape enemy torture devices:
↓

Pinchy dress shoes are the worst torture. I'd design a large dress shoe that secretly conceals a comfy, fuzzy slipper!

How to detonate explosives safely: →

← Watch out! Cleo's about to blow!

How to cross dangerous minefields:
↓

precarious puzzle pieces

stinky laundry
↓

careful — possible spills

slippery hazards

small, sharp projectiles

not-to-be crumpled homework

Mom thinks Life Skills sounds like a great class. When she went to school, she had to take Poise class. One of the things she had to do was walk around with a book on her head for good posture. (No wonder Life Skills sounds good to her!) Only the girls had to take the Poise class, and they also had Cooking and Sewing while the boys had Wood Shop. Definitely unfair! At least now we're all taking the same stuff together. I guess that's an improvement. Now we can all be miserable.

I tried the book-on-the-head trick, and it was actually kind of fun. More fun than sewing will be, I bet!

Is this what it means to have a head for books?

Once Mom starts talking about the "old days," she can't stop.

can you believe it? We were graded on our fingernails! I flunked "cuticles" because my moons didn't show.

And if you chewed your fingernails— watch out!

fingernail

This lighter part here is the "moon." Who cares if it shows?

Last night at dinner, Cleo acted like <u>she</u> was taking Poise class — she chewed with her mouth closed the whole time, and she wasn't loud or obnoxious. She was actually <u>dainty</u>!

The NEW Cleo!

She said "please" and "thank you."

She dabbed her mouth with her napkin.

She took small forkfuls, not globs shoveled on.

She sipped her milk instead of chugging it down.

Mom even noticed. She gushed over how polite Cleo was and said I should follow her example. But I'm already plenty polite! <u>I</u> don't chew with my mouth open or gulp down milk. I absolutely don't need lessons from Cleo on ANYTHING!

Something's up. There's got to be a reason Cleo's acting this way. She's never been normal before. Why pretend she is now?

It was a puzzle I had to solve.
↓

good manners   +   Cleo   =   What?

I don't call this spying. It's a scientific experiment in audio enhancement.

empty paper-towel tube — or low-tech listening device

door to Cleo's room

I get it! I know why Cleo's suddenly so polite. She's eating lunch at school with Oliver now, and she doesn't want him to think she's a rude slob. I heard her talking to Gigi on the phone.

Oh, Gigi, isn't he the cutest! I hope he'll ask me to the dance . . .

So there's a <u>dance</u> at her school! If Oliver saw the real Cleo, there's <u>no way</u> he'd ask her to go with him. And if I were her, I wouldn't want to go anyway. How will she know how to dance without looking goofy? They should teach dancing in Life Skills instead of sewing. That's the kind of thing you really need to learn, but it's too embarrassing to ask for help. Are you just supposed to copy what other people do? What if they're all crummy dancers, too? Then you'd look like a goon!

Follow the footprints for a crash course in dancing!

Wrong or right? Who can say?

Sewing is the first thing we're doing in Life Skills, and there are three good things about it. One, Carly and Maya are in my class, so we can suffer together. Two, I love all the cute things we sew with — the buttons, bobbins, thimbles, and needle threaders (but I'd rather play with them than _sew_ with them). Three, the sewing machines are high-tech, with lots of cool features (a blend of computer and sewing machine). The bad thing is actually sewing. No sewing machine is so high-tech it could do all the work for me, and I'm definitely all thumbs. In fact, I'm afraid I'll sew my thumb by mistake.

It looks like a meek, mild-mannered machine, but once you turn it on, that needle keeps on stabbing!

needle threader — it's too pretty just to thread needles

Hee, hee! Just put your thumb RIGHT there!

buttons like a computer keyboard for all the different kinds of stitches — backstitch, zigzag stitch, button stitch, side stitch, stitch in time

I love all the buttons — they're like tiny treasures.

Unfortunately, sock puppets are not a choice for a sewing project.

yarn hair

button eyes

thumb mouth

Hello, Footsie! Seen any interesting toes lately?

There are lots of sewing projects we can do. All the girls are making clothes. The boys are sewing anything <u>but</u> clothes.

the girls' projects:
↓

a pleated skirt (Maya picked this.)

a vest (Carly picked this.)

a bicycle messenger bag (Brandon picked this — I bet his mom helps him.)

a duffel bag (Seth picked this, the easiest boy choice.)

a blouse (This is for the really ambitious like Charisse. She already knows how to sew.)

I picked this.
↓

a Halloween costume (Max picked this.)

but it a jumper — I'll probably never wear it, looked like the simplest thing to make.

This may not be Poise class, but it's just as useless.

It's not about sewing — it's about <u>learning</u>. Just do the best you can.

It <u>is</u> about sewing. It's fun, and you can make cool stuff.

Mom

Carly

Is sewing a life skill because you have to figure out how to deal with everyone's opinions?

I think my head will explode! Why can't sewing just be about sewing? Then I'd be happy making place mats or sock puppets. They're at my level. Anyway, why is sewing a "girl" thing? A girl thing should be anything a girl wants to do — and this girl doesn't want to sew!

Oliver came over again today. Cleo was absolutely disgusting with him. She's wearing mascara now and acts like a completely different person around him.

She even holds her body differently and tilts her head all the time as if someone told her it made her look better. Is Oliver fooled by the fakey-fake Cleo? He must be or he wouldn't be here. I should slip him a note warning him of the truth.

Save yourself! Cleo is actually a monster in disguise. The person you _think_ is Cleo doesn't really exist. Escape while you can!

This time Cleo and Oliver were doing their math homework together. How sweet! Cleo can act dumb about math _and_ science!

When he left, Oliver smiled at me and said, "See ya, Amelia." Maybe he _will_ let me come to the science fair! I felt bad I hadn't really given him that note — he's much too nice for Cleo! She's still mad at me. She said the next time Oliver comes over, I'd better make myself scarce. I would if she'd stop acting like a jerk!

What is it with you anyway? Why are you acting so different? Why are you pretending to be dumb? Do you think boys only like stupid girls? And fakey-fake ones?

Mind your own beeswax, Amelia! You don't know anything about boys!

I had to write to Nadia about what's going on.

Dear Nadia,
Cleo's been even ~~wierder~~ ~~weirder~~ ~~wierder~~ weirder than usual. She likes this boy, and when he's around, she pretends she's stupid. Cleo's a lot of things, but dumb isn't one of them. She acts all sweet, too, and really fake. Is that how you have to be to get a boy to like you? I wonder if that's why Mom divorced Dad — maybe she got tired of being fake all the time. Don't boys like normal girls?

Save me from spelling this word!

FLEET FEET XPRESS 40¢

Nadia Kurz
61 South St.
Barton, CA
91010

luv, Amelia
Yours till the friend ships!

Maybe I'm not a normal girl anyway. If girls are supposed to be good at sewing, why am I so terrible? I ruined my zipper three times today and had to start over.

Charisse is already half finished with her blouse, even though Max keeps interrupting her, asking her for help with his costume.

Max can't fool me — I recognize that goo-goo-eyed look. He doesn't want help from Charisse, he wants her attention! →

Um, Charisse, um, I was just wondering if...

← Max isn't pretending to be bad at sewing. He really is bad! But why does he think being bad at something will make Charisse like him? Could Cleo be right?

Just a minute, Max, and I'll be happy to help.

← I don't know if Charisse gets it or not, but she's always nice and helps him. Does that mean she likes him back?

I asked for help, too — not from Charisse, but from Carly. Her vest looks beautiful! Too bad she doesn't fall for helping the weak the way Oliver and Charisse do. She said I've got to do my OWN work.

Why is sewing called a "domestic art"? If it had to do with art, I'd be better at it. And if it's domestic, does that mean it's not wild, like a domestic animal? If it's tame, why can't I control a zipper?

swatch of fabric from Carly's vest ←

The only person who's worse at sewing than I am is Charlie. He refuses to sew <u>anything</u> because he thinks sewing is "girly." I'm sure tired of hearing that! I don't see why pushing a needle through cloth is so feminine. I think Charlie just wants an excuse not to sew.

How NOT to sew a zipper: ↓

crooked so the teeth don't mesh

Mr. Bipka didn't buy Charlie's reason, either. ↓

It just so happens, Charlie, that MANY famous clothing designers are men — and they all sew. Haven't you heard of Calvin Klein and Tommy Hilfiger?

not following ↑ the edges of the opening

So maybe it's not that I'm not girly enough to sew well, but that I'm <u>too</u> girly! ↑

all bunched up

But to make Charlie feel better, Mr. Bipka said we'd start a new project while we're still working on our sewing. He promised we'd use real tools, like hammers and nails, not just needles and thread. I wonder what we'll make? Whatever it is, it's got to be better than a crooked, bunched-up jumper.

My jumper looks like a monster costume more than a dress — I'll be more of a Frankenstein than Max! →

the 10-year-old daughter of Frankenstein ↙

Cleo's acting "girlier" than ever. I never really thought of Cleo as a girl before — I just thought of her as Cleo. But now it's like she has a neon sign flashing over her head saying "GIRL, GIRL, GIRL."

glitter hair gel

Am I imagining things, or is she actually pluckin her eyebrows?

zillions of bracelets to make up for not having pierced ears

Is part of growing up getting more girly? Maybe this isn't an act — maybe Cleo will stay this way forever. But Mom's a grown-up, and she definitely doesn't act girly.

Am I going to act like that when I get older? That's a scary thought! I wish Nadia would answer my postcard. I'm not sure what to think anymore.

Will this be me?

head empty of any interesting ideas because I'm so busy pretending to be dumb

fluttering eyelashes (but then I can't see well enough to read or write!)

sparkle dust on my cheeks

bracelets that clink and clank so much that I get a headache when I try to draw

I'd rather NOT grow up if this is what will happen!

Today when Oliver came over, Cleo actually fluttered her eyelashes at him — I thought that only happened in cartoons! I thought I'd see big pink hearts pop up over her head.

flutter flutter

Oh, Oliver!

Hey, do you know why the elephant crossed the road?

It was the chicken's day off!

Whenever Cleo gets gushy, Oliver starts telling jokes, and he's actually pretty funny. I hate to admit it, but I like him. I don't <u>like</u> like him, of course. And I'd NEVER act dumb to get his attention. I think it's better to act smart — or act regular, which <u>is</u> being smart.

When he was leaving, I said, "Bye, Oliver!" but my voice was too loud and squeaky. I sounded like a broken doll. I don't care if Oliver likes me, but I've g<u>ot</u> to do something so he takes me seriously — and takes me to the science fair!

I've been too busy thinking about girl stuff when I should've been thinking about science. Test tubes are <u>much</u> more interesting! →

Father Time ↓

The clocks make me think of sayings with time in them, like "Time's up!" Why not "Time's down?"

↑ tick ↓ tock

Or "in the nick of time." How does time nick you? It's not sharp.

For use with a small cut, scrape, or nick of time.

I may not be making any progress with Oliver, but I took a definite step forward in Life Skills class. I put aside my jumper for now (phew!) and started on the new project — making a clock. We're not making the actual mechanical stuff inside the clock, just the wooden box around it. We have to saw the wood, drill a hole in one piece, hammer it all together, and decorate it. Then we stick the clock hands through the hole and leave the little clock motor on the other s

← When we're finished, it'll look something like this. Now THIS is the kind of project I like!

Mr. Bipka was enthusiastic about sewing, but he LOVES tools.

Tools are your friends. Treat them with care, and they'll serve you well. If you're rough with them, they won't work for you. Remember — respect your tools!

a measuring tape

carpenter's level

It looks like a simple screwdriver, but to Mr. Bipka, it's a miracle device.

To me, it's a hammer. To Mr. Bipka, it's a best friend.

At least with the clock project, we're all making the same thing. The only difference is in the decoration.

← girl   clocks ↗

↑
I wonder where mine will fit in?

← boy clocks ↗

I must be treating my tools well, because my clock's turning out O.K. I'm still deciding how to decorate it, though. I want it to look really good to make up for the bad grade my jumper will get — if I ever finish it.

I begged Carly one last time to have pity on me and my poor jumper. →

> Pleeeeeease, you're my last chance! You don't have to do it for me — just show me how to sew the zipper right. Pleeease!

Finally she said yes!
↓

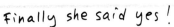

> Oh, all right!

> Just because you're so pathetic.

> Thank you, thank you, thank you, thank you, thank you, thank you, thank you, thank you, thank you!!

> And you're my best friend.

> You can even borrow my jumper whenever you want! It can live in your closet!

> Uh, thanks, Amelia, but NO, thanks!

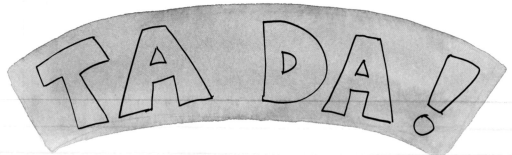

TA DA!

I thought it was going to be a great day because I FINALLY finished sewing that zipper, but I was wrong. Mr. Bipka made a special announcement, and it was an especially <u>horrible</u> announcement.

mouth of doom ↓

Class, you've done <u>such</u> a <u>super</u> job on your sewing projects that I have a SPECIAL surprise for you!

At the end of the month, we're going to put on a FASHION SHOW for the <u>whole</u> school! You'll model the wonderful things you've made, and everyone will have a chance to admire your work.

The class didn't exactly jump up and applaud (except Charisse). Me, I just felt very, VERY sick.

Charisse ↓   Charlie ↓

I've always wanted to be a model!

Model clothes! That's definitely a girl thing — count me out!

Maya ↓

It could be fun.

My vest did turn out pretty good.

Charisse will look terrific!

Carly →

me ↓

Count me out, too — I feel queasy!

↑ Max

At dinner, Cleo turned back into her regular nasty self when she heard about the fashion show.

gloating Cleo →

> I wish we went to the same school, just for that day! I'd love to see you model your — what is it? A handkerchief? A place mat? Or is it a pillowcase? That seems your speed!

Then Cleo had her own announcement, and she turned all sugary sweet.

> I have some news myself. I'll be going to the dance next Friday night with Oliver. Then Saturday, we're going to the awards ceremony for the state science fair!

That does it! I might get over looking ridiculous at the fashion show, but I won't get over not going to that awards ceremony! I've got two weeks to show Oliver how good I am at science so he'll invite me. (And that'll show Cleo that acting smart beats acting dumb any day!)

Today Gigi came over (not Oliver!). I thought she'd be mad at Cleo because they'd planned on going to the dance together if Oliver didn't ask Cleo. They were even working on a song they were going to sing together onstage.

They were going to dress up in red, glittery blouses and call themselves the Marshmallow Sisters. Fortunately for the rest of the school, Oliver changed that by asking Cleo to go with _him_. So instead of practicing their song, Cleo and Gigi practiced dancing.

Gigi says she understands why Cleo picked Oliver over her best friend, but I sure don't!

Is this a dance or a sumo wrestling pose?

Even though she's not singing, I'm already embarrassed for Cleo. She dances like she's losing her balance.

Finally, a postcard from Nadia! ↘

Make a Wish!

WISHING WELL

Dear Amelia,
I don't have an older sister,
~~so~~ I don't know if Cleo's normal
or not. But she's never been normal
before, so why should she be now?
What's the point of having someone
like a fake version of you anyway?
Then it's not _you_ they like, but
~~someone else~~. I promise I won't
be like Cleo when I'm older,
no matter what!

luv, Nadia   yours till the friendship rings!

Amelia
564 N. Homerest Pl.
Oopa, Oregon
97881

Nadia's right. I plan on getting better when I'm older, not worse. I'll be better at writing, drawing, _and_ science (maybe even better at math, too).

For now, I've got to be smart enough to think up a good invention to impress Oliver. I'll prove to Cleo that the brain is mightier than the fluttering eyelashes!

possible inventions
↓

mysterious chemical
that makes Cleo sweet
for real

shoes that dance for you
so you never look like a
jerk

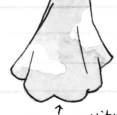

cloak of invisibility so
no one sees how ugly your
clothes are (O.K., I admit I
got this idea from Harry Potter,
but who says you can't get
ideas from books?)

I know these are all _dream_
inventions, but I could make
something using my clock —
if I finish it in time. (A clock
should _always_ be done in time, after
all. Clock ... in time. Get it?)

Sewing was even worse than usual today. All I could think about was what kind of invention I could make, so my mind wasn't exactly on my jumper. At least I managed to finish it (if you call _this_ finished).

Somehow I messed up the armholes. Now it's more like a straitjacket than a jumper.

↓

How can I wear this? It's not clothing — it's a torture device!

And if I've failed at sewing, have I failed at being a girl? Is Cleo right? Is something wrong with me? (I _know_ there's something wrong with my jumper!)

Carly tried to cheer me up.
↓

It's not so bad, Amelia. If you accessorize — you know, wear a nice scarf, maybe a belt — no one will notice the mistakes.

I'd have to wear a gorilla mask to distract people from those _mistakes_.

Then Max said that since my jumper is so scary-looking, I may as well wear his Frankenstein costume with it to make a really horrible monster. I snapped back that he could wear my jumper, since he thought the two went together so well. (But I'm afraid he's right. Even without a mask, that jumper will make me look like a horror creature.)

Mr. Bipka
s right —
r. Hammer
my friend —
haven't
+ my
umb once!

Even Charisse had to make a comment.

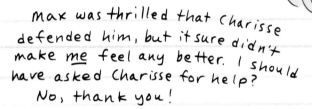

Just because you don't sew well, don't take it out on Max. You should have asked for help.

Max was thrilled that Charisse defended him, but it sure didn't make me feel any better. I should have asked Charisse for help? No, thank you!

Thinking about my jumper just makes my stomach hurt. I've got to work on my clock instead and get started on my invention for Oliver. I only have a week!

I can cut it with Ms. saw!

At least the clock is fun. I'm actually good with tools — I'm not messing up at all. I'm so far behind, though, that some kids have started on the next project — bicycle repair. Charisse really hates this one. She can't stand getting oil on her hands and smelling all greasy. So she says bike repair is a boy thing.

s weren't rough th Mr. Sandpaper. →

Carly, who's an expert at bikes <u>and</u> sewing, just laughs at her. "Saying it's a boy thing is just an excuse," she tells Charisse. "What you <u>really</u> mean is that it's not <u>your</u> thing. You're not every girl, you know." That gave me an idea for a quiz.

The Truth Behind Boy and Girl Things

Circle all answers that fit.

To make a product for girls, you add:

a) pink or purple   c) eyelashes
b) lace or ribbons   d) flowers or hearts

To make a product for boys, you add:

a) lightning bolts   c) camouflage colors
b) guns or knives   d) race cars

Correct answers: <u>none</u> of the above. That's what companies <u>think</u> boys and girls like. But they're wrong. All girls aren't the same, and neither are all boys. And even if <u>most</u> girls like something, I don't have to like it, too.

Carly likes sewing AND working with tools. →

That doesn't make her <u>less</u> of a girl than Charisse. And I'm not, either!

I told Cleo about The Truth Behind Boy and Girl Things. I told her she didn't have to act so dumb and girly to get Oliver to like her. It wasn't exactly what she wanted to hear.

As if you'd know anything about it, twerp!

But I do know. At least I think I know. And I've got some ideas now for my Oliver invention. I'm just not sure what the whole thing will do yet. Meanwhile, I've finished my clock!

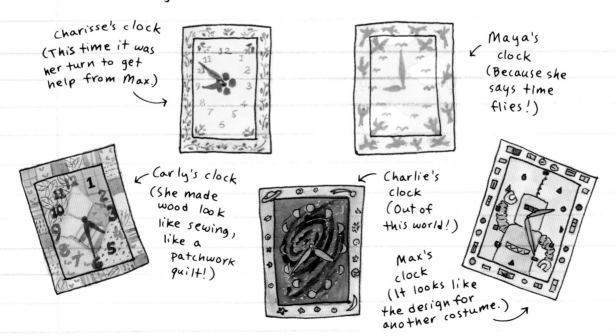

Charisse's clock (This time it was her turn to get help from Max.)

Maya's clock (Because she says time flies!)

Carly's clock (She made wood look like sewing, like a patchwork quilt!)

Charlie's clock (Out of this world!)

Max's clock (It looks like the design for another costume.)

my clock — I call it "Time to Get Cooking!" I may not be proud of my jumper, but I'm very proud of my clock. →

← In fact, this clock does more than tell time — it just gave me a **GREAT** idea! _Now_ I know what to make to impress Oliver!

I call it the "Egg-O-Matic." Here's how it works:

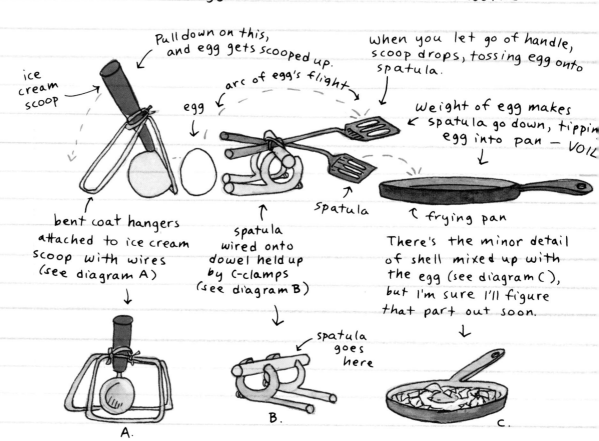

Pull down on this, and egg gets scooped up.

arc of egg's flight

when you let go of handle, scoop drops, tossing egg onto spatula.

ice cream scoop →

egg ↓

Weight of egg makes ← spatula go down, tipping egg into pan — VOILÀ

↓

← Spatula

↖ Spatula

↖ frying pan

bent coat hangers attached to ice cream scoop with wires (see diagram A)

spatula wired onto dowel held up by C-clamps (see diagram B)

There's the minor detail of shell mixed up with the egg (see diagram C), but I'm sure I'll figure that part out soon.

↓   ↓   ↓

A.

spatula goes here

B.

C.

I figured this out just in time — tomorrow's Cleo's big dance, so Oliver's coming over. And I've got the fashion show tomorrow, too. I've got to make the Egg-O-Matic work and show Oliver how much I deserve to go to the science fair awards. Otherwise, with the fashion show, and me dressed like a mutated pumpkin, tomorrow will be the worst day of my life.

Tick! Tick! Tick!

The clock is counting down how long I have, and time is running out!

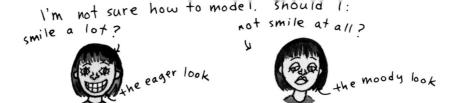

I'm not sure how to model. Should I:
smile a lot?
the eager look

not smile at all?
the moody look

In class, Mr. Bipka didn't let us work on ANYTHING. He was too busy organizing the fashion show. Everyone had to practice modeling. Charisse swung her hair a lot, Max clomped like a monster, and Carly was her usual graceful self. Even Maya was smiling, like it was fun, but I felt as clumsy as Cleo dancing the Funky Chicken. The boys kept laughing like it was the goofiest thing to do, but I couldn't laugh with them. I was too worried everyone would be laughing at <u>me</u>.

Then Mr. Bipka made an announcement that saved my life.

Class, we need one person to be announcer for the show. Unfortunately, the announcer will not be able to model.

Is anyone willing to give up modeling and try announcing?

Should I:

alk slowly?
↓

ng pause — tap

run to get over with?
↓

ph, galumph

<u>All</u> the boys wanted to be the announcer — and so did I. We took turns reading a sample description.

Everyone was supposed to write their own description. I hadn't even started mine yet, but naturally Charisse had hers done.

Here's a lovely blouse modeled by the lovely Charisse. This satin creation with cap sleeves and velvet-covered buttons is a dream come true!
Thank you, Charisse!

Most of the boys couldn't get through the first sentence without giggling. Max completely cracked up. Charlie said so many "ums" you could barely um-derstand him. Only Brandon read the whole thing through without any mistakes. But this was my one chance to be saved from certain doom, so I did more than read well — I read with FEELING. I read like I was the emcee for the Miss America pageant.

I tried to stay calm, but I was all sweaty and nervous.

beads of sweat — it was do or die!

lips parched with worry

AND MR. BIPKA PICKED ME!!!

Charlie was great modeling his messenger bag.

He rode his newly repaired bike onstage and even popped a wheelie. The audience loved it!

The fashion show turned out to be fun. Mr. Bipka gave me extra credit for announcing, which I really needed because the jumper only earned me a C-. I guess I did learn something in Life Skills class — it's not whether it's a girl thing or a boy thing that matters, but whether it's YOUR thing!

Today turned out so good, I'm sure my Egg-O-Matic will wow Oliver, and tomorrow I'll get to go to the science fair!

DISASTER!

Well, Oliver doesn't think I'm a baby anymore — he thinks I'm an idiot! When he came over to pick up Cleo, she was still in the bathroom, knee-deep in all the makeup she was putting on. Perfect, I thought, I can show him the Egg-O-Matic. Mom was asking all the usual grown-up questions — "Do you like school? What's your favorite subject? Did you brush your teeth?"

Finally, Oliver noticed my invention. "What's that?" he asked.

"Oh," I said, "a little something I've been working on. I like to invent things."

"Really?" he said.

"Really," I said.

"So what happens when you pull down this lever?" he asked.

"Try it," I said.

He did.

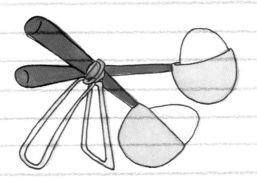

The scoop part worked perfectly, but instead of flipping the egg onto the spatula, it acted like a catapult.

And the egg cracked right on Oliver's face!

Mom was furious! She apologized over and over to Oliver, but nothing helped. He was so embarrassed and upset that he went right home — without even seeing Cleo. It was a good thing Mom sent me to my room because when Cleo heard what happened, she ERUPTED! I thought she would break down my door and strangle me.

The bedroom door shook so hard, I thought it'd break! Cleo only stopped when Gigi came over, and the two of them went to the dance without Oliver.

chair under doorknob in case lock won't hold

me, cowering behind my bed

teeth chattering

knees knocking

I felt bad for Oliver, bad for Cleo, and bad for me!

I didn't sleep much last night. I felt so bad about ruining Cleo's big night. All I could do was apologize when she finally woke up.

I didn't mean for Oliver to get egg on his face. I'm so so SO sorry!

Cleo was pretty groggy, but she wasn't mad anymore. In fact, she looked happy.

Cleo perked up.

Was the dance fun at all?

Yeah, you know, it was. After I stopped trying so hard to be dainty, Gigi and I took off our shoes and danced together. We moved, girl!

Cleo smiled at me! That doesn't happen very often.

I liked her talking to me that way — it felt like she was letting me in on the secret of how to survive high-school dances. Now that's a life skill. Then she said something that REALLY surprised me.

Gigi and I even did our singing act, and you know who was there when we got offstage? Oliver! He'd gone home to clean up, and he still wanted to dance with me. He even liked my singing — he likes me, my regular self.

And he thought your egg contraption was pretty clever. He — I mean, we — want to know if you want to go to the science fair with us. Maybe you'll see how to make a better Egg-O-Matic.

Good old Cleo — back to talking with her mouth full! And she was being nice for real, not fakey nice.

Now it was my turn to be nice — for real.

No, Cleo, you guys go on your own. I almost ruined the dance for you. I don't want to mess this up, too.

Besides, I'll go to the state science fair someday on my own, when I've got a project in it. Then I'll invite you to be _my_ guest.

In fact, I've got an idea right now for a GREAT invention — the automatic egg wiper. First it launches the egg, then it wipes it off. I just need to work on the last part, and it'll be perfect!